The Potters' Kitchen

The Potters' Kitchen

by Rachel Isadora

Greenwillow Books
A Division of William Morrow & Company, Inc. • New York

 Inquiries should be addressed to Greenwillow Books, 105 Madison Avenue, New York, N.Y. 10016. Printed in the United States of America.

1 2 3 4 5 6 7 8 9 10

Library of Congress Cataloging in Publication Data

Isadora, Rachel. The Potters' kitchen. Summary: The Potter family moves from the country to the city and makes a happy adjustment. [1. Moving, Household—Fiction. 2. City and town life—Fiction] I. Title. PZ7.1763Po [E] 76-47666

ISBN 0-688-80089-0 ISBN 0-688-84089-2 lib. bdg.

For Samantha and Jonathan Sohn

and Robert

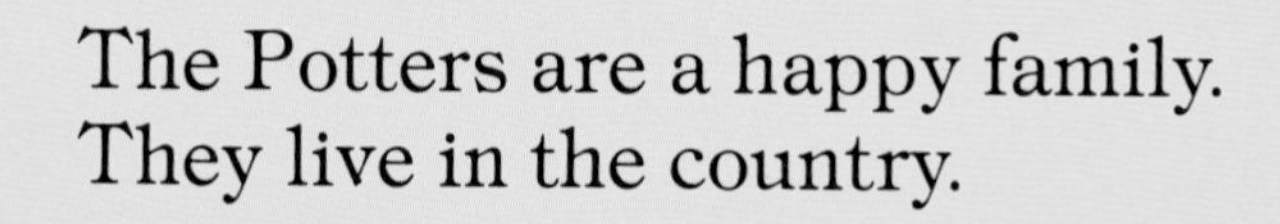

The Potters are a happy family.
They live in the country.

Potters

The kitchen
is their
favorite room.

The kitchen is a busy place, especially in the evening.
Samantha and her friends help Mrs. Potter prepare dinner.

Jonathan and his friends play outside and Mr. Potter works in his garden until dinner is ready. Then everybody comes in and the kitchen is warm and noisy.

There are also times when the kitchen is quiet.

One evening, after dinner, Mr. Potter tells
the children that he has a new job in the city.
They will have to move.

Everyone is sad when the time comes
to say good-bye.

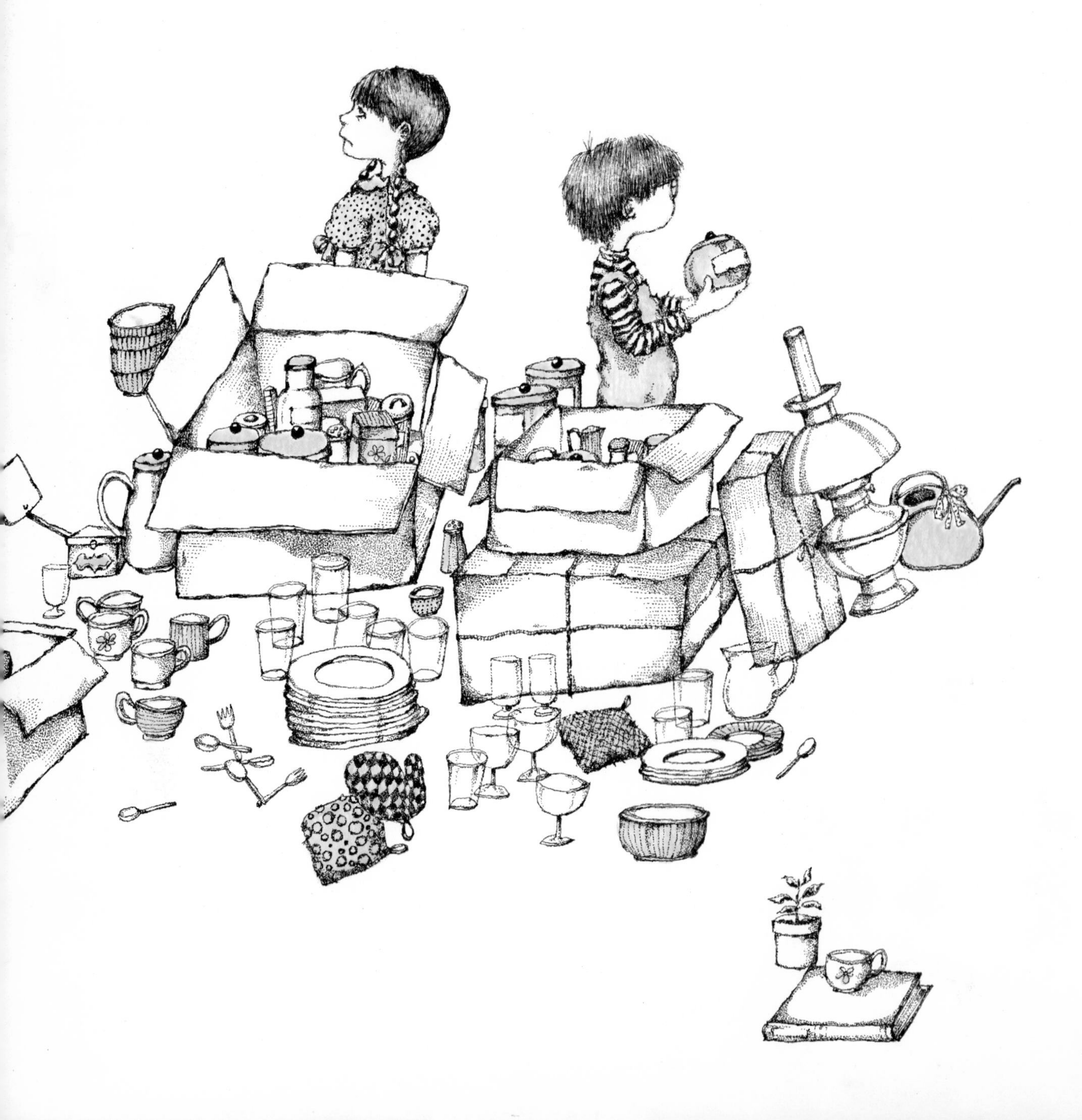

The Potters move
to an apartment
in a tall,
tall building on
a very busy street.

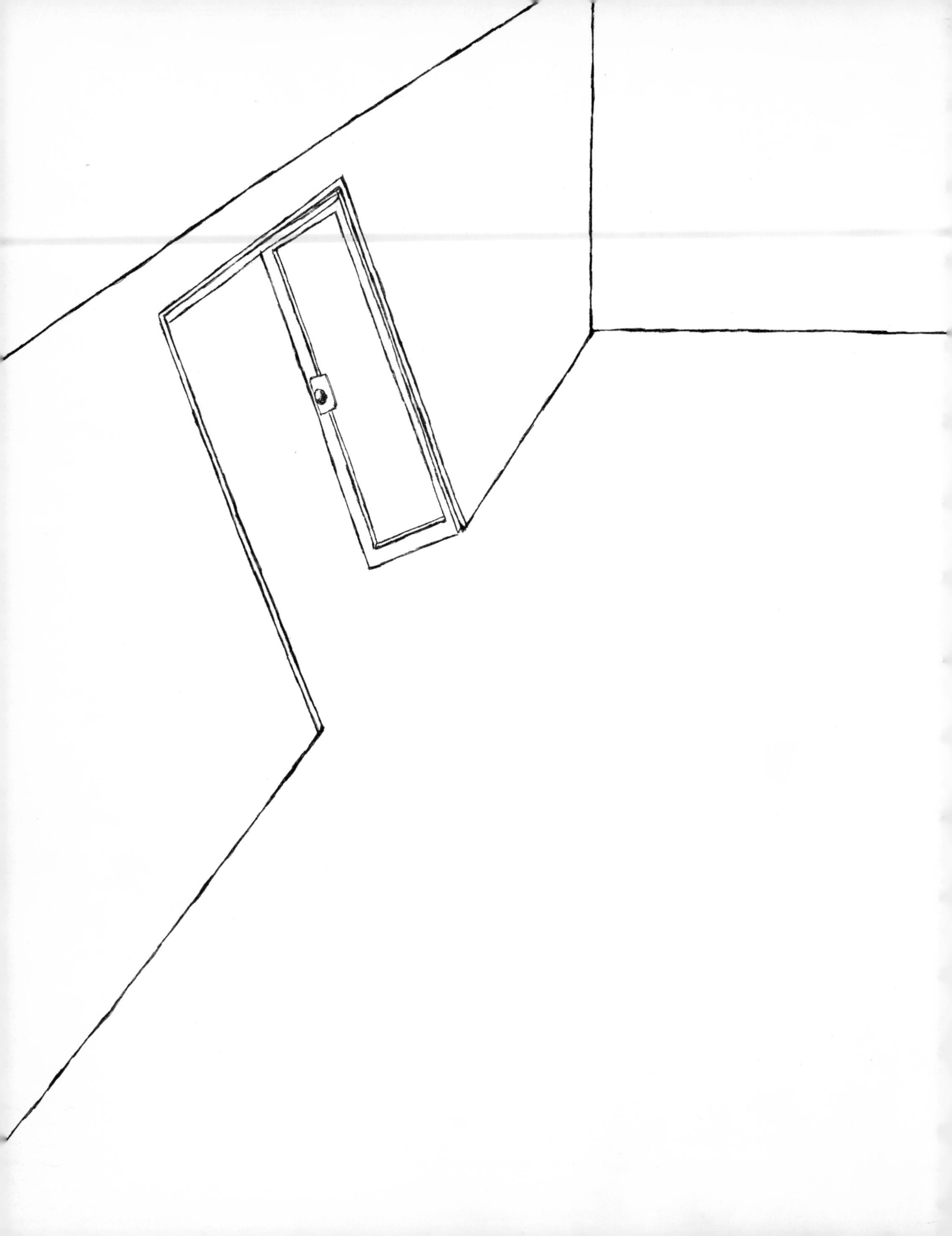

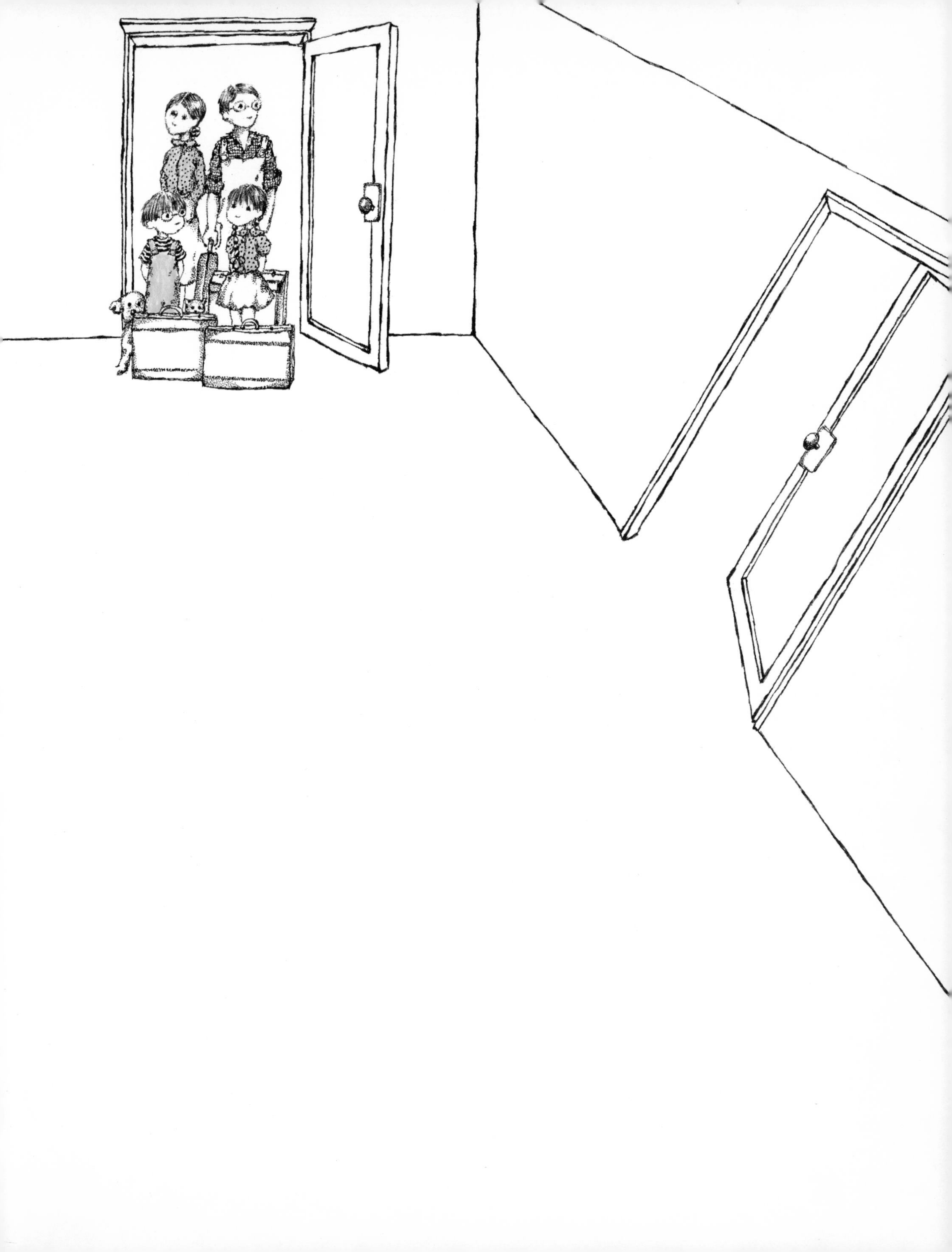

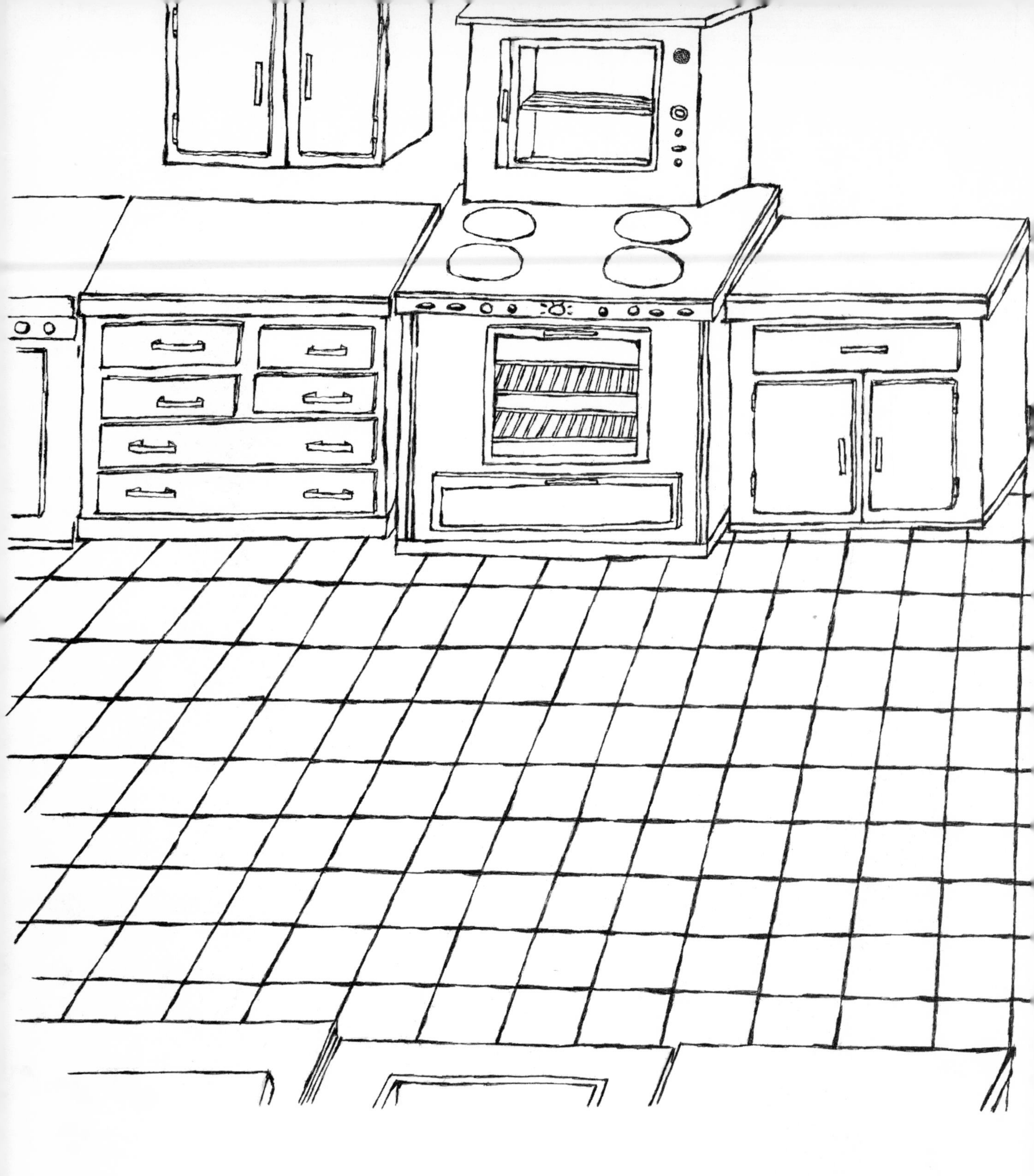

The kitchen is big and shiny and new,

but it is not at all like their country kitchen.

In the morning
Mr. Potter leaves
for work.
Samantha
and Jonathan
have nothing to do.
"Why don't you
go down
and see what the
playground is like?"
Mrs. Potter suggests.
Samantha goes,
but Jonathan
doesn't want to.

Samantha makes a friend.

When they get tired of playing,
Samantha brings her new friend home.

In the afternoon Mrs. Roberts and her son Ben
drop in to welcome their new neighbors.

Mrs. Potter invites Mrs. Roberts to have coffee.

And Jonathan and Ben have lollipops.

Before they know it, it is time to prepare dinner.

And Mr. Potter comes home.

It is their first dinner
in their new kitchen.
Everybody starts talking at once.
There is so much to tell about.

The Potters live in the city.
They are a happy family.